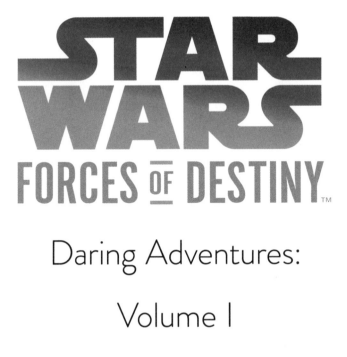

STAR WARS

FORCES OF DESTINY™

Daring Adventures:

Volume I

Written by
Emma Carlson Berne

DISNEP

LUCASFILM
PRESS

Los Angeles • New York

Printed in the United States of America

First Edition, August 2017
3 5 7 9 10 8 6 4
FAC-029261-17283
Library of Congress Control Number on file
ISBN 978-1-368-01122-8

Visit the official *Star Wars* website at: www.starwars.com.

SUSTAINABLE
FORESTRY
INITIATIVE

Certified Sourcing

www.sfiprogram.org
SFI-01415

CONTENTS

REY

SANDS OF JAKKU

A Message from Maz:

I am glad you have come to see me, my friend. Come close! Don't be shy. This is my favorite place. Look around you. See the deep starry sky? I have lived a long time. But I have never grown tired of watching the stars, here by my fire, sitting on a rock by the lake. And I have tea. Here, help me sprinkle the leaves into my kettle. You must pinch them, like so. It brings out the flavor. Spiced nysillim—delicious.

Now we have our tea, you and I, and we

have the fire, throwing its orange sparks into the night sky. I know what you have come for— stories, eh? Tales. Yes, I see that I am right. And, oh, my friend, I have tales to tell, stories about true heroes. I've certainly known more than a few around the galaxy. Lean close. And listen—learn what it takes to be a hero. And remember, the choices we make, the actions we take, the moments—both big and small—shape us into forces of destiny.

CHAPTER 1

Rey strode through the Jakku desert, her boots sinking into the sand soft as powder, staff slung on her back. The little astromech droid she'd just rescued, BB-8, rolled by her side. Teedo had picked up the droid and tied him in a net on the side of his luggabeast. Teedos were unpredictable, so it was lucky this one had listened when Rey told him to drop the astromech. You never knew with them.

Rey glanced down at the droid, his spherical body rolling along with his little head balanced on top. He was smeared with dirt, but at least his bent antenna was fixed—thanks to Rey.

"How'd Teedo find you?" she asked him.

The droid whirred at her briefly.

Rey snorted. "Oh, classified. Got it. Big secret."

BB-8 beeped softly.

Rey paused. She couldn't remember the last time she'd heard a thank you from someone.

"You're welcome," she said stiffly.

BB-8 sped up by her side and let out a gentle buzz.

Rey glanced down at the round droid. Without realizing it, she'd been speed walking toward the AT-AT she called home. She slowed her stride.

"Sorry, little guy," she said. "I'm not used to walking with someone else."

That was true, she reflected. She was always alone—whether she was working, selling her scrap to the junk dealer Unkar Plutt, or at home in the AT-AT. Even when she was around others, like in Niima Outpost, she was still alone.

Until now.

It felt odd, walking through the desert with someone else after so much time alone. Odd, but not bad. Actually, it felt kind of nice. Like having a friend. Or family.

But the sky was darkening to dusky purple and she was hungry. Unkar Plutt had given her only one quarter food portion for her junk that day, even though she had found especially valuable starship parts. Rey stopped and bent down.

"Niima Outpost is northwest from here, okay?" She pointed out the distant crags that marked the village.

"It takes me a couple hours on my speeder. It'll take you longer, but the terrain is flat. Just hold straight and you'll hit it eventually."

She looked down at the droid's little white

head, and a funny feeling rose in her throat. She swallowed it down and patted him firmly.

"Take care, okay? And watch out for nightwatcher worms. The old scavengers say the worms can sense the vibrations in the sand—track people who might be parking ships or speeders. Then they eat the junk. There are a lot of them around here."

She'd never seen a whole nightwatcher in the flesh—few had. Some people called them sandborers. One old scavenger called them Arconan night terrors. They usually stayed under the sand. But once or twice, coming back from a late run, she'd seen a pair of big red eyes, blinking at her from just above the surface. That was the nightwatcher worm, and though

Rey knew she wasn't in danger, her speeder and her net of junk were. She always shivered and hurried on. She didn't want any of her stuff to be that thing's meal.

BB-8 beeped indignantly.

"I know you're not junk, but they might mistake you for it anyway, so just be on the lookout, okay?" Rey turned on her heel, willing herself not to look back.

A whirring sound came from behind her. Rey stopped and turned around.

BB-8 stood alone in the vast desert, his head drooping. He looked at her and let out one sad little beep.

Rey sighed. "Okay. Okay! You can stay with me. Just for tonight! I'll take you to the outpost in the morning."

CHAPTER 2

BB-8 rolled happily by her side as the massive
Jakku sun slid below the horizon, burning
orange and red. The AT-AT rose like a lump
in the distance. Rey's stomach rumbled and
she thought of the food she had eaten earlier.
A quarter portion. She had to find a way to get
more.

The whirring stopped and she realized BB-8 was no longer by her side. Rey turned. The droid was staring at something in the sand.

"Beebee-Ate, come on!" Rey called.

The night wind kicked up, whipping strands of hair in her face. "We don't want to be out on the plains after dark."

The droid beeped urgently.

"Wait. What do you see?" Rey stopped short, her pulse quickening.

Two red lights popped up from the sand. Just as quickly, they disappeared. Rey's hand crept toward the staff on her back. Delicately, she slipped the strap off her shoulder and

 tightened her hands around the staff, holding it ready.

"Don't move," she muttered. "Just. Don't. Move. That's a nightwatcher worm. I told you, it feeds on junk."

The droid let out one frightened squeak. Then he kept perfectly still.

Rey held her breath. The eyes popped up again. She could see the head now—like an upside-down triangle with the two blinking eyes sticking out at either end.

They waited. Rey's heart was pounding so hard she wondered if the nightwatcher could hear it. She could almost *feel* its long, coiled body waiting under the sand where they stood. A moment stretched out, long and quiet. BB-8 remained frozen. Not even his antennae quivered.

The sand rippled. The red eyes zoomed toward them.

"*Now* we run!" Rey shouted. She sprinted as fast as she could toward her AT-AT home, BB-8 rolling along quickly at her side.

The soft sand slipped and slid under her feet and she stumbled, almost falling. BB-8 pushed himself against her and for an instant she clung to his round head.

"Thanks!" Rey gasped. "You're a true friend."

BB-8 beeped as his whirring accelerated into a high-pitched whine.

The ground rolled again as the nightwatcher rumbled under the sand.

"It probably hasn't eaten today! Hurry! We need to find something else to feed it!"

Rey's mind raced. The AT-AT would do the trick. It had plenty of rusty beams and panels. The worm wouldn't need much. They would just have to get there in time.

Suddenly, the worm shot into the air ahead of them like a starship blasting out of the sand. BB-8 slid to a halt, beeping frantically. Rey pulled up, whipping her staff in front of her and the droid. Her eyes bulged. The scavengers hadn't lied—the worm was massive. Its shiny, plated coils heaved as it whipped its head around. The blinking eyes drew a bead on them and Rey sucked in her breath.

"BB-8! This way!" she shouted.

BB-8 sped up, bumping Rey and almost knocking her into the sand.

The worm whipped into the air and landed on the sand with a slap. It shot toward BB-8. The droid let out a high-pitched whine as he zigzagged, trying to avoid the worm's gaping black maw.

The worm lunged and snapped, missing BB-8 by centimeters as the droid sped across the sand.

Rey waved her staff as high as she could, hoping to draw the worm's attention.

"Hey!" she screamed. "Over here! Look!"

The worm's head swung in her direction and it paused. Rey and BB-8 held perfectly still. Then the worm sank back under the sand as if sucked into the depths of the earth.

Silence. BB-8 rolled close to Rey's side and

pressed against her. Rey listened. No sound except the whisper of the evening breeze.

The droid beeped quietly.

Ffoom! Before Rey could answer, the worm exploded out of the sand, writhing against the twilit sky.

CHAPTER 3

"Nope!" Rey shouted. "Actually, it's not done with us! Let's go!"

They took off toward the AT-AT again. *Faster, faster, come on!* Rey screamed silently. Her breath whistled in her chest, and cramping pains shot up and down her side. The worm slithered behind them, scraping over the sand.

BB-8 wasn't next to her. Where was he? Rey

whipped around. The little droid stood alone, as if frozen. The worm loomed over BB-8, its jaws wide, its tongues wiggling, poised to strike.

"Not today!" Rey shouted, and just as the creature lunged forward, she shoved her staff vertically into its jaws, cramming the weapon hard against the roof of its mouth and sensing instead of hearing its screech of pain and surprise.

Immediately, she regretted the move. Now she had no staff, which meant no protection. Rey shoved BB-8.

"Get going!" she ordered.

Rey shot a glance over her shoulder as they ran. The worm was thrashing back and forth with the staff holding its mouth open. She could see the staff bending, more, a little more, into a U-shape. Suddenly, the staff shot out of the worm's mouth.

Rey flung herself forward, grabbing at the staff. The spinning stick thumped into her hands and she landed neatly, feet apart, body poised.

"Aaand—thank you! Keep moving, BB-8!"

BB-8 beeped as he rolled.

The worm disappeared again, burrowing

and racing, the sand rippling above it like a river. The AT-AT was nearer—Rey could see its familiar shape silhouetted against the sky. Rey put her head down and clenched her teeth, charging toward it. They were almost there. Almost to the walker—almost to the junk that would satisfy the worm.

The sand moved like an arrow—the worm was tracking them underground. Rey stopped and turned sharply, hoping to throw the creature off. But the rolling sand headed straight for BB-8.

"BB-8! Wait! No!"

But before she could grab the droid, the worm erupted out of the sand and, in one swift movement, grabbed BB-8 in its jaws and sucked him down under the surface. The droid's panicked beeps were suddenly silenced.

"No!" Rey screamed. She forced herself to stop running. Still—she had to stay still. She wasn't going to lose her new friend to a hungry worm. She closed her eyes, drew in a big breath, and let it go. She imagined her mind focusing down to a narrow pinhole of light. She thought of nothing but the worm. Where was the worm? The worm didn't want to hurt BB-8. It was just an animal. It was hungry. It was another living thing, and it just wanted to find food, like she did. She and the worm were the same, sort of.

Rey felt a twinge of compassion for the hungry worm and, suddenly, a thin thread

flung itself like a lifeline from her mind—
straight to the worm. There! It was right by the
AT-AT—right by the junk!

Panting, Rey ran to the spot on the ground
where she sensed the worm was. Rey raised
her staff in the air. The stick felt like part of
her body. It would do her bidding. The staff
plunged down into the hot sand.

Thunk! The staff hit something hard—the
worm's head. The worm reared out of the
ground in front of her, knocking Rey off her
feet. It rose mightily into the sky, thrashing its
head back and forth, its red eyes glowing. BB-8
was clenched in its jaws, but the droid was still
functioning. Rey could see his lights blinking.

Rey charged forward. She wasn't thinking;
she was all bone and muscle. The worm's head

snaked along the ground toward her. This was it, right now, before it disappeared again.

"Hang on, Beebee-Ate!" Rey shouted. She jammed her staff into the worm's open mouth, wedging it behind the droid's body. The worm whipped its head around and Rey almost lost her grip as its blue saliva flowed over her hand.

BB-8 beeped faintly for help.

"Hang on!" Rey said again.

Rey grunted as she pushed on the staff. The worm's jaws were clamped tight, but the droid's round body was slippery. If she could just pop him out . . . Rey gave a mighty shove on the staff and BB-8 suddenly sailed out of the worm's mouth, arcing through the air and landing with a thump on the sand.

The worm snapped its jaws closed and shot

across the sand toward its lost prey. Her breath whistling in her ears, Rey raced to BB-8, picked him up, and with all her might hoisted him on top of a rusting part of her AT-AT home, where he landed with a hollow *thunk*. She scrambled up behind him.

The nightwatcher looked up at them, its massive body quiet. It looked almost sad.

"Stay back!" she cautioned the slime-covered droid, and worked her staff behind some rusted panels—one, two, three. A beam clattered down with the panels. That was good; it could have that one, too. And another one fell. Rey shoved the junk onto the sand, right at the worm's face.

"Here! I know you're hungry. Take this!"

The worm sank into the sand and sucked

some of the junk under, devouring it. Rey crouched beside BB-8 and listened to the crunching and gnashing under the sand. BB-8 still dripped blue goo.

"Okay?" Rey whispered to him.

The droid whirred softly.

"I'm glad that goo is your only problem." Rey put her arm around BB-8, and together they watched the sand as the buried worm sucked down the last panel.

"We're safe now." Rey let out a breath. She straightened slowly, feeling as if she'd been pummeled all over.

"Welcome to Jakku," she told BB-8. Rey held up her staff, also coated with worm slime. "How about we clean up a little?"

The droid beeped twice.

"How did I find you under the sand?"

Rey hesitated. *Concentrating.* It was hard to explain. She'd never told anyone about it before.

"I'm just lucky, I guess." Then she grinned at the astromech. "Unlike you, my little friend."

The droid spun rapidly, splashing a string of blue nightwatcher goo across Rey's face.

"Hey!" Rey wiped the goo off with her arm. "Watch it!"

The droid beeped and rolled forward. Rey followed, smiling a little to herself. She jumped lightly onto the sand and set BB-8 down beside her.

"Now, let's go get you cleaned up."

The AT-AT hatch was just ahead—home, some food—and funny . . . a friend, too.

Friend. She liked the sound of that.

CHAPTER 4

The last of the night stars were still visible in the western sky when Rey opened the AT-AT hatch the next morning. She took a deep breath, savoring the lingering moments of dampness before the sun rose. The pearl-gray sky soared over the rolling expanse of sand. The eastern horizon glowed rose pink.

Rey turned back and called, "Beebee-Ate, come on! You're all charged up. I'm rested. Let's get going."

She felt a twinge even as she spoke. It had been kind of nice having company for a night— even nonhuman company. Still, the droid's owner had to be found.

BB-8 rolled out of the AT-AT and over to the speeder, where Rey was fastening on a stronger net. She didn't want the droid falling out over the sand.

"We're heading for Niima Outpost," she
said, taking a clip from her belt and fastening
the net to the speeder.

The droid whirred eagerly in response.

"I know you're anxious to complete your
mission." Rey hoisted the droid into the net
and tightened the clips.

"If someone's looking for you, we'll find
them at the outpost. Everyone on Jakku turns
up there eventually."

Rey suddenly looked up, something
catching her eye. She squinted at the horizon.
There it was again—a flash of light. She
reached into the pouch at her waist and pulled
out her old quadnocs. She'd traded for them in
town the previous year. The automatic tracker

was faulty, but they still helped her spot things far away.

BB-8 beeped questioningly from the net beside her.

"I don't know what it is—yet." Rey spun the tracker dial. She spotted a small cloth-wrapped figure on an idling speeder bike on the horizon, buzzing up and down, waiting.

"Teedo . . ." Rey dropped the quadnocs back into her pouch. "He's back for his prize. We've got to go."

Rey reached up to mount the speeder, but before she could, BB-8 let out a warning alarm.

Rey whirled around just in time to see two of Teedo's thugs running toward her. She caught a glimpse of rag-wrapped faces and big goggles as she whipped her staff off her back and thrust it under one of the thug's legs. He grunted as he hit the sand. Rey shoved her staff into the net and leapt onto her speeder.

"Let's get out of here!" she shouted to BB-8 as she cranked the accelerator.

The engine rose to a whine as they picked up speed, the orange sand flowing like a rippling ocean beneath them.

BB-8 beeped to her over the sound of the engine.

"Glad you like the speeder!" Rey yelled. "I built it myself! I don't think anyone else could drive it—it's really cranky!"

She shot a glance over her shoulder.

The thugs had gotten on their own bikes and soon both they and Teedo were catching up fast. The whine of their smaller speeders rose to a scream as they pushed the vehicles to their limit.

BB-8 beeped frantically. All his lights were on and his body was whirring pointlessly in the net.

"Stop fretting!" Rey punched the accelerator and her speeder shot ahead. "I've got this covered."

The speeder couldn't go faster, though. There was no way to outrun them.

"Hang on." She slowed, bouncing BB-8. He beeped indignantly.

Teedo and the thugs swung up on either side of Rey's speeder, yelling at her in their gruff tongue. Rey glanced left and right. The smaller speeders swung in to ram her.

"Here we go!" she shouted, and bracing herself, she hit the brake hard.

The speeder dropped downward sharply and the thugs crashed into each other. Rey shot ahead just above the sand, glancing behind her. A thrill of satisfaction rose in her when she saw the wreckage of the two small speeders piled like so much twisted metal, black smoke rising from the mess.

BB-8 beeped encouragement from his net.

"Thanks," Rey exhaled. "I didn't think it was a bad job, either."

She straightened up a little, keeping the speeder on course, and wiped her forehead with her sleeve.

"That's two down. Now it's just Teedo left."

He was following on his speeder not far behind. Unfortunately, he was a much better driver than his buddies.

"Come here," Rey murmured. She powered down the speeder slightly, hoping to get Teedo to come closer. At the same time, she cruised toward a crashed Star Destroyer just ahead.

Lured by the slower speed, Teedo sped up until he was just behind them.

"Now, how about this?" Rey muttered as she suddenly accelerated.

The big speeder shot forward, dangerously close to the edge of the destroyer.

Rey aimed her speeder along the perimeter and grabbed her staff from the net. She dragged it along the edge of the destroyer.

Zing! A piece flew off and crashed into Teedo's speeder. She heard him curse as he ducked, but he held his course. *Zing!* She knocked another chunk of the ship toward Teedo, then another.

BB-8 let out a warning alarm as metal bounced off his head.

"Sorry, buddy," Rey answered.

Just ahead, a big panel hung loose. Rey kept the speeder steady with her knees and gripped her staff in both hands.

"Uggh!" she grunted as she knocked the panel off with the help of the speeder.

The panel fell onto Teedo, almost knocking him off his bike and forcing him to slow down.

"Finally!" Rey guided her speeder ahead, with the wind whipping through her sweaty hair.

"Turns out you're quite a popular droid! Everyone wants to either eat you or take you apart."

The droid beeped at her.

"Yes!" Rey said. "Exactly like with that nightwatcher worm. Let's go pay him a visit."

BB-8 beeped nervously.

"Yes, I'm sure it's the best idea. And Teedo's right behind us, so let's go."

CHAPTER 5

Rey leaned into her speeder, swooping around
the big hull of the Star Destroyer, looking for
an opening.

"There!" She spotted a black hole and
swooped through.

It was quiet and shadowy inside the ship's
hull. Wind whistled through the opening

above. The sand had blown in for many years, making a thick bed inside.

"Don't panic, but this is a nightwatcher worm den. One of the old scavengers told me about it."

Rey circled slowly above the ground.

The droid whirred loudly in his net.

"I *am* your friend." Rey brought the speeder down gently on a metal outcropping just above the sand.

"Trust me. Didn't I rescue you before? You think I'm going to just let you get eaten after all that trouble?" Rey crouched beside the speeder.

"Just wait for it! And don't make any more noise. No sense in attracting a nightwatcher before we have to."

Just then, a crashing, clanking noise came from overhead, along with the *brrrr* of an engine. A shadow darkened the entrance and Teedo tore down into the ship. He pulled up short when he saw them, and Rey leapt down from the ledge.

She put her hands on her hips.

"If you want the droid, Teedo, you're going to have to come and get him. Let's see if you can," she goaded.

BB-8 let out several loud beeps from his net.

"*Shhh!*" Rey hissed. "Didn't I say to trust me?"

Teedo lowered his bike to the sand and parked it, watching Rey all the time. She could tell he suspected something—he just didn't know what. Slowly, Teedo walked toward the edge where BB-8 dangled in his net. A blaster was in his hand.

"Come on," Rey breathed. "Come on, little worm. Nice junk for you here. Nice junk."

If her plan was going to work, a worm would have to detect their presence before Teedo reached BB-8. She had made the droid a sitting duck. Teedo walked a step closer, never taking his eyes off the droid. He raised the blaster. The sand under Rey's feet stayed still.

"Come *on*," she whispered. Teedo took another step. He suspected a trap. Another step. Rey's heart pounded in her ears.

Then, under her feet, a ripple, then a rumbling. A worm!

"Time's up, Teedo!" Rey shouted, just as the worm burst through the sand, mouth gaping, and jerked Teedo's speeder into its jaws before slithering back under the sand.

Teedo scrambled up the hull, frantically clinging to the bits of metal and wire as he grappled toward the opening overhead.

He pulled himself up and out, and a moment later, his footsteps pounded on the outside of the hull over their heads.

Rey smiled as she mounted her speeder and kicked it into high gear.

The droid let out a string of loud beeps at her side.

Rey did a loop around the side of the destroyer and shot out into the sunlight.

"Teedo will be fine!" she yelled to BB-8. "But he is going to need a new bike.

"Thank you!" Rey called back to the worm. "Enjoy your meal!"

She aimed the speeder at Niima Outpost, and together, she and BB-8 flew over the sand, straight toward the rising sun.

SABINE
THE NEWEST RECRUIT

A MESSAGE FROM MAZ:

Here, let's have another cup of tea. See? I
finished mine so quickly. You too? Let me heat
the kettle again on the coals. Now hold out your
cup. I'll fill yours, then mine. Oooh! Too hot!
I've burned my tongue. Here, I'll put our cups
in the grass. The night dew will cool them. It
just goes to show you, sometimes we need to

be patient, when dealing with tea—or with our friends. We want the best for them even when they can't see it themselves. But letting them make their own decisions is what a true friend does, no? And sometimes just being a friend can make you a hero. . . .

CHAPTER 6

"Ketsu Onyo!" Sabine Wren whirled from the *Ghost*'s control panel and stared at Hera, the Twi'lek leader of Phoenix Squadron.

"Ketsu is willing to help us with this mission? Great! We could use her skills."

Ketsu was Sabine's oldest friend from the Imperial Academy, but they hadn't parted on the best terms. Ketsu took up with a criminal group called Black Sun—a rough crowd. She showed up trying to steal a droid carrying intelligence while Sabine was on a rebel mission. In the old days, the two of them had worked like one mind in separate bodies. But Ketsu seemed different when Sabine saw her again—harder, angrier. They almost dueled, and Sabine had wondered if Ketsu might really kill her. But then they were discovered by Imperial forces. With their old combination of guts and brains, they had escaped—together.

Ever since, Sabine had hoped that Ketsu might come back, work with the rebels. She'd been pressing Hera to get Ketsu on a good rebel mission—to convince her that she had a place in the Rebellion.

Hera turned from the radar screen, her brow creased.

"Ketsu has left Black Sun. I know her skills are considerable. But you will remember that Ketsu was not ready to join the Rebellion when we last met her. If she has changed her mind, she hasn't told me. She is willing to help us with *this* mission. But that's all she would commit to."

They were nearing Garel City, where the mission was to secure food rations for those in need.

"I'll drop you near the spaceport. You'll meet Ketsu there."

Sabine nodded and sighed. "All right," she said. "I understand."

Hera calmly steered the *Ghost* through space. Below them, the lights of Garel twinkled brighter and brighter as they approached the planet. She kept an eye out for a hangar where she could set down the *Ghost* and spoke without turning.

"It is not always easy to convince someone to join the Rebellion, Sabine. Remember that. Remember how you yourself had to be convinced. She must have the will to join with others to increase her strength—something you need to remember, as well, since you hold yourself away from others so often."

She spun around and fixed Sabine with a stern look. Sabine dropped her eyes.

"Ketsu is used to working alone, and only

for profit. I don't know if she will give that
up—yet."

Hera turned back to the controls.

"Garel City approaching. Prepare to land
for mission drop-off."

CHAPTER 7

The crates were poking her in the back.
Sabine reached behind her and shoved one out
of the way. That entrance to the Garel City
Spaceport was fairly deserted, which was good
because there weren't many places to hide.
Sabine turned the thought of her old friend
Ketsu over in her mind. Ketsu was tough,
unapologetic, and ruthless. She'd bounced

around plenty—working for the Empire, then as a bounty hunter, and finally for Black Sun. Maybe this mission would convince Ketsu that the next group she should be a part of was the Rebellion.

Sabine scanned the area. A cleaning droid whirred by, carrying a mop. She looked at her chrono. Ketsu was late and Sabine was getting more and more cramped in her hiding place behind the crates. Maybe Ketsu wasn't going to show. Maybe she'd decided she didn't want to be part of the mission after all. Sabine sighed. Maybe she wasn't going to get to work with her old friend again.

The cleaning droid finished whatever it was doing and whirred off. The place was empty, and still no Ketsu. *Looks like this'll be a solo mission after all,* Sabine thought. She activated her comlink to let Hera know. Her fingers felt heavy, like her heart. She raised her wrist to her mouth. Then a slender figure clad in black suddenly landed beside her in a graceful crouch.

"Ketsu!" Sabine resisted the urge to throw her arms around her friend. Instead, she slapped her on the back. She looked the same as the last time Sabine had seen her. Thin and tough as wire, with her dark hair shaved on the sides. "I didn't see you coming in."

Ketsu gave her usual grin.

"That's because I'm good."

"Black Sun taught you that?" Sabine asked.

Ketsu's mouth twisted. "Let's just say, their methods weren't always ones I prefer. I figure

I work best alone. But I wanted to help on this mission."

Sabine pretended to be checking her blaster.

"You know, Ketsu, you don't *have* to work alone. You can join the rebels. We want you in the family."

She eyed her friend sideways. Sabine had always been able to see the softness under Ketsu's hard surface.

Ketsu's brow furrowed and she stuck out her jaw.

"I'm fine. I don't need another family, okay? Let's just get on with the mission."

Sabine grinned. "All right. All right. Let's see if we still have that old magic."

She stepped out from behind the stack of crates and, with Ketsu close behind, gingerly pressed a button for the door set into the back wall of the spaceport. Ketsu motioned to the door—which remained closed.

"It's not opening, Wren," she whispered.

Sabine glanced around to make sure no one was watching them. They had to get through this door, then into the restricted section inside. That was where they would find their target. But the place was crawling with stormtroopers. She glanced down at her and Ketsu's scarred and dented armor. Sabine's was covered with her own wild designs. They didn't exactly blend in. Sabine hoped they could do this without being spotted.

Sabine thumbed the door's activation button again. Nothing. It was locked, of course.

"Hang on, let me try to bypass this." She crouched by the panel next to the door and started pressing buttons.

Ketsu looked left and right.

"Forget that. Stand back, will you?" She pulled out her blaster. A flash of blue light exploded from the end, leaving a neat smoking hole in the door. "No code needed."

"Not when you're around, apparently." Sabine put her hand through the hole and activated the door from the inside.

"Now let's get in there before someone comes to investigate."

They walked inside the spaceport, the

door sliding shut behind them. They were in a central holding area, vast and stacked with more crates on all sides. The place was deserted—for the moment. Almost immediately, Sabine spotted a restricted door with a bright-yellow emblem at the end of the enormous space. Blasters out, she headed toward it, with Ketsu covering her back.

"This is feeling pretty familiar, doing this together," Sabine said. She advanced steadily on the door.

"Just what I was thinking. Some things you never forget."

Something skittered in the corner, and Ketsu swung around, staff ready.

"Ahhh, just a mouse or something."

Sabine punched in the activation code on the keypad beside the door that led to the restricted area.

"Now that you've left Black Sun, your armor will need a repaint."

The door beeped and slid back. "I could do that for you."

She'd always painted her own armor. Ketsu would remember.

"You'll need it if you do join the Rebellion full-time, you know."

"I appreciate that, Sabine. But like I said, I'm just not sure I'm ready to join the rebels yet. I'm used to working on my own, you know. That's a hard habit to shake."

Sabine looked around. The room was filled with more boxes, but she still didn't see the mission target. A dark, narrow hallway led away from the room. It looked like they'd have to enter it to find what they were looking for.

"Easy now," Sabine murmured.

They both knew that the deeper into the spaceport they moved, the more stormtroopers would be around.

They stepped into the hallway, but immediately Ketsu yanked Sabine back. Two heavily armed stormtroopers passed across the end of the hall. When the stormtroopers were gone, Sabine nodded at Ketsu and they entered the hallway once more, making their way down the passage into a small room with armored walls and loading doors at one end.

"We're here. Hera said the cargo would be at loading bay nineteen." Sabine eyed the doors.

"We'll have to get through the doors to get the food."

Ketsu came up beside her. "Food for the Rebellion? I'll admit this isn't the kind of mission I had in mind. I didn't exactly picture myself liberating some food scraps. How about taking down some Imperials instead?"

Sabine inspected the doors. They were heavily fortified with strips of durasteel across a thick frame.

"Well, it's not always about combat. Sometimes the mission is about helping people in need."

She eyed the activation panel. There was no telling what would be behind the doors. They'd have to be ready. She drew her blaster.

"Next time, pick a mission with a little more kick," quipped Ketsu.

"Okay, this is it." Sabine punched in the activation code. The doors hissed open.

The mission target, a specific crate, was there, all right, just like Hera had said. And so was a group of stormtroopers, surrounding the crate and pointing blasters straight at the women.

CHAPTER 8

"Maybe I spoke too soon about that kick!" Ketsu shouted as they both flung themselves sideways behind a pile of metal panels.

Pew! Pew! The stormtroopers fired, the blasts ricocheting off the panels. Ketsu stuck her head up for an instant, fired off several blasts, then ducked down.

Sabine aimed at the lead stormtrooper and

hit him square in the back. He fell to the floor with a clatter.

"Nice!" Ketsu yelled.

The troopers rushed the pile they were hiding behind and Ketsu rose up, Sabine right behind her, firing with two blasters now. Ketsu moved across the floor, blasting bolt after bolt. She caught another trooper under the chin and he crumpled.

Sabine grabbed one of the metal panels and held it up as a shield as she fired at a trooper moving in on Ketsu. The blast caught the edge of the food crate and the front of the crate fell open.

The crate wasn't just full of rations. A little refugee Chadra-Fan boy crouched inside, his eyes wide with fear, a half-eaten ration bar dangling from one hand. He must have been in the middle of his snack when the shooting started.

"A stowaway! Oh, this just got a lot harder!" Sabine yelled to Ketsu.

Sabine eyed a trooper circling her slowly, aiming his blaster.

"You wanted exciting, old friend? Now it's a rescue mission! That do the trick for you?"

"Absolutely!" Ketsu suddenly rushed the group of stormtroopers, getting one with a roundhouse kick.

"Sweet dreams!" she grunted, elbowing another in the chin. He hit the floor hard, his helmet clanging against the ground. A trooper fired and Ketsu's blaster arced through the air. She was disarmed!

The stormtrooper laughed. "Too bad," he said, and took aim.

Suddenly, a bolt of blue-white fire shot past Ketsu's shoulder and hit the trooper square in the chest.

"Thanks!" Ketsu shouted to Sabine. "I'll get the kid—cover me!"

"Got it!" Sabine yelled back. She fired on the troopers steadily, deflecting their blasts with her panel shield. Ketsu raced toward the crate and pulled the crying child out, cradling him to her chest as Sabine covered her back. Ketsu dove behind the crate, still holding the boy. Sabine snatched Ketsu's blaster from the ground and flung it at her friend. Ketsu's hand shot up from behind the crate and caught it.

Sabine crouched behind the opened

doors where they'd come in and thumbed her comlink.

"Spectre-Two! We could use some help in here! The mission's gotten a lot more complicated!"

Thank goodness, Hera was on the comm. Sabine breathed a sigh of relief when she heard Spectre-2's strong voice. She knew she could count on Hera.

"On our way, Spectre-Five."

Sabine suddenly saw a trooper creeping up to the crate, blaster aimed.

"Ketsu!" she shouted.

Ketsu shoved the crate to the side and flung herself in front of the boy, shielding him. The trooper's blaster fire hit Ketsu in the shoulder. The boy yelped with fear. Ketsu fired at the trooper, but thanks to her injured shoulder, her aim was off.

Her friend needed an assist, Sabine could tell—and now. Wriggling like a snake, she slid over to the crate on her belly, propped herself up on her elbows, and blasted the trooper between the shoulder blades. He crumpled to the floor with a grunt.

"Hang on, guys!" Sabine yelled. "Hera's on her way!"

Ketsu looked at the troopers closing in around them. "And just how long until she gets here?"

Her words were lost in the roar of massive engines. Seconds later, a gray ship swooped down from above. Exhaust and engine steam filled the air.

Sabine grinned. "Not long!"

The *Ghost* fired a blast from its cannon as the back hold ramp lowered. The droid Chopper beeped at them to hurry.

Sabine wanted to hug the battered orange-and-white astromech droid. Instead, she grabbed the little boy in her arms. Ketsu let off blast after blast at the remaining troopers to give Sabine cover.

"Go! Go!" she shouted.

Crouching, Sabine ran toward the *Ghost* with the little boy bouncing over her shoulder. Blue-white streams of light zinged by her head as she ran up the boarding ramp

and scrambled into the hold. Ketsu, firing over her shoulder, flung herself into the ship as Chopper hit the button to raise the ramp.

Sabine braced herself and the boy as the *Ghost*'s massive engines fired up and sent the ship soaring into the sky.

She exhaled. They'd done it. They'd rescued the boy. Ketsu looked over from her position by the door. Her face was smeared with soot and the shoulder of her armor was marred with blast marks, but the old, familiar grin lit her face.

"We did it, partner," she said. Sabine lifted her hand in a high five.

Then the little boy struggled to his feet, holding the wall for balance.

"Thank you," he said in a high, musical voice. He snuffled through his little bat-like snout. Sabine ruffled his hair.

"No problem," she told him. "Hey, go on up to the bridge. Chopper will take you. You can see how this thing flies."

The little boy's face broke into the first smile they'd seen from him since they found him, and he ran off into the ship with the droid whirring behind.

Hera strode into the hold, a smile on her face.

"Nice work, team," she told them, hands on her hips. "I

thought the two of you would be stronger together."

"It was fun, working together again." Sabine rested her arms on her up-drawn knees.

"I'm glad I could still be a teammate to you, Wren," Ketsu said in a low voice. "I . . . I wanted to be."

Sabine looked over at her old friend while Hera watched them both.

"You were. You really were a teammate. I couldn't have done it without you. Hera was right. Two can be stronger than one."

"How about you, Ketsu?" Hera broke in. "How did it feel fighting for the Rebellion?"

A grin cracked Ketsu's sooty face. "You know, it didn't feel all that bad. Being a part of something that fights for good—it's been a long time. Too long, I think."

Sabine smiled back at her friend. "I think so, too."

CHAPTER 9

"Stop fidgeting!" Sabine crouched over Ketsu's shoulder, painting in short, swift strokes.

"I'm almost done." She swiped on the last coat of yellow and set down the brush.

"There!"

Ketsu craned her neck, and together they looked at the Phoenix Squadron symbol painted on her armor—over the spot where the Black Sun mark had once been. Ketsu exhaled.

"It's perfect."

She stood up, straight and tall, and offered her hand.

Sabine faced her friend and slapped her hand into Ketsu's.

"Welcome to the Rebellion."

PADMÉ
The IMPOSTER INSIDE

A MESSAGE FROM MAZ:

Our fire is getting low. I have some wood there, my friend. Put on a few sticks. Pine. They will crackle in the night and send up showers of sparks to light our way. We've been talking so long our tea got cold! Put your hand on my cup—cold, isn't it? You stoke the fire. I'll heat this last bit of tea.

As I was saying . . . sometimes, small deeds are what really matters. These simple gestures can be the kindest. And that kindness— well, that can make you into a hero. Doing something for a friend can be the most heroic gesture of all.

CHAPTER 10

Padmé hurried along the white marble corridor of the Jedi Temple on Coruscant, her footsteps echoing off the soaring walls and high, open ceiling, her purple cloak floating behind her.

Ahsoka Tano's quarters were at the end of the corridor.

I hope she agrees to help me, Padmé thought. *I need her.*

Padmé stopped in front of the closed door and knocked twice on the smooth metal.

"Yes?" Ahsoka's familiar voice came from within. "Please come in."

Padmé slid the door open. "Ahsoka, I came—"

She stopped. "Oh! I'm sorry. I didn't know you were meditating."

Ahsoka sat very still in the middle of the room, cross-legged on the floor. A thin sleeping  pad covered neatly with a blanket, a side table, and a simple cabinet were the only objects in the room. Sunlight streamed through the open blinds on one wall.

"I am finished now," Ahsoka said, opening her eyes. She rose to her feet.

"It's so good to see you, Senator. But I'm surprised you've come here to the Temple. Is everything all right?"

Padmé shook her head and strode to the window. She looked out at the busy Coruscant streets below.

"No, I'm afraid it isn't. Tomorrow, I am giving a dinner party for the Arthurian delegates."

"And you want me to keep an eye out?" Ahsoka asked.

"Just a quick check of my building beforehand," Padmé said.

"It shouldn't take long. I know it's a big favor—"

"Not for you," Ahsoka said, cutting her off.

"You've been on my mind lately, Padmé. I've heard about the possible assassination plots against you. And I'm happy to help. But you have Captain Typho. Surely he can secure the premises."

"No, I want you." Padmé took Ahsoka's hand in hers.

"I need the talents of a Jedi, and I trust you completely. Besides, you're the best. You're very skilled, you know. Please. As a favor to me."

Ahsoka paused, then nodded.

"Of course, Padmé. I would be honored to protect you."

Padmé exhaled. "Thank you, Ahsoka. You are generous. This event is very important. Nothing can go wrong."

CHAPTER 11

The next evening, Padmé looked up from
the platter of fruit she was arranging in the
kitchen. There were footsteps on the stairs.
Ahsoka must be done checking outside the
building. The Padawan had already finished
her check of Padmé's home and declared it
safe.

Padmé nestled the last berries into place and walked out of the kitchen, the platter in her hands. The spacious blue rooms almost glowed in the golden light from the setting sun. Outside the floor-to-ceiling windows, the skyscrapers of Coruscant glittered like spears of crystal.

Inside, soft music played and the scent from various arrangements of flowers, placed on every surface, filled the rooms. Padmé glanced at a mirror on the wall. She was glad she'd decided to wear the simple cream-colored jumpsuit with the matching cape. Her hair was drawn back in a sleek bun.

"Padmé?" Ahsoka came in the open door. "I just finished securing the outside of the building. Everything is clear."

She quickly rubbed at a streak of dirt down the side of her tunic. Padmé pretended not to see. She could tell Ahsoka sometimes felt out of place in elegant surroundings.

Padmé smiled and placed the platter on the long dining table, which sparkled with expensive goblets and plates.

"I appreciate your helping me, Ahsoka." She smiled.

"These negotiations with the Arthurian delegates are critical, and there are a lot of people who don't want them to happen. You know, it might not be such a bad idea if you stick around."

Padmé followed Ahsoka's gaze as the Togruta girl glanced around the apartment at the big roomy couches, the handwoven rugs, the carved wood side tables rubbed to a soft glow. Bowls of fruits and sweets were elegantly arranged on a long side table, where a server in a simple black robe was setting up a vase of lilies and vines. Ahsoka shook her head.

"Thank you, Padmé, but it's not really my place to mingle with politicians."

Padmé opened her mouth to press the issue, then nodded and took the girl's hand instead. "Next time then. I insist." Ahsoka looked both relieved and disappointed. She bowed her head in respect and turned toward the door. Then she stopped. Padmé frowned.

"What is it?"

"The table. Something is strange about the table."

Ahsoka stepped toward it, studying its contents, then looked back up at Padmé.

"Why did you set it with utensils? The Arthurian delegates never use them and might find it insulting."

Padmé glanced at the long dining table. The Padawan was right. Forks, knives, and spoons were at each place setting.

"I'm not sure why the utensils are out. I was very specific in my instructions not to use them."

Padmé could see Ahsoka's body tense up.

A little zing of tension ran through Padmé.

"Excuse me!" she called to the server woman in the black robe.

The woman turned and drew a blaster. For a long moment, no one moved. Then Ahsoka grabbed Padmé, pulling her behind the table, and the server fired.

"Padmé? Is she on the guest list?"

"No, she is not!" Padmé shouted, and leapt back as Ahsoka threw her arm across Padmé, just as the woman ran toward them, her face twisted into a snarl—and then twisted into something else. The server's face suddenly transformed into that of the shape-shifting bounty hunter Cato Parasitti. Ahsoka shoved Padmé backward toward the wall and flung herself in front of the senator. Padmé gasped, her heart pounding.

Cato lunged forward with frightening speed. Padmé had encountered Cato before but had forgotten how fast the bounty hunter could move. Ahsoka threw herself to the right and grabbed Padmé, still pressed against the wall. Pain throbbed through Padmé's elbow as Ahsoka once again threw her behind the big dining table.

"How did she—" Padmé tried to say, but the rest of her words were drowned out when Ahsoka grabbed one of the wooden chairs and hurled it at Cato. The bounty hunter tangled with the chair for an instant—all the time Ahsoka needed to draw her lightsabers.

Padmé, weaponless, crouched behind the table. Her hands itched for her blaster. The bounty hunter, her own blaster in hand, fired once more.

"Uhhh!" Ahsoka ducked, the blast barely missing her. It shot into the drapes and they burst into flames.

Ahsoka ignited both her lightsabers as Cato fired off another blast. Ahsoka deflected it with a swift upward jab—a move Padmé suspected Anakin had taught her—and walked forward, swinging the lightsabers in front of her as Cato fired blast after blast. The air filled with smoke from the burning drapes.

Sweat ran down the sides of Ahsoka's face. Grunting, she forced Cato back step by step. Cato drew a small object out of a pouch on her belt.

Padmé crept forward through the debris. If she could get to Cato from behind, knock her down—suddenly, she spotted something large and gray attached to the underside of the table. Padmé stared at it, her eyes stinging from the smoke. It was a cube, metal and blinking with red lights. She placed her hand on it and felt a vibration, deep inside, as if the cube was ticking. Suddenly, she knew what it was—and what Cato was holding.

"Ahsoka!" she screamed, running her hands over the cube, looking for a button, a latch, anything. The Togruta girl whirled around.

"A bomb!" Padmé shouted. "She's planted a bomb! She's holding the detonator. I can't disarm it!"

CHAPTER 12

"Send it to me!" Ahsoka shouted.

With all her strength, Padmé pushed the table toward Ahsoka.

Ahsoka brought her lightsaber down on the table, slicing a circle around the bomb. She concentrated and Force-pushed the cut-out bomb across the room and through one of the big windows.

A massive explosion shook the room as the bomb exploded outside in midair. Behind Ahsoka, the bounty hunter whirled and ran for the exit.

"The door!" Padmé shouted, alerting Ahsoka.

Ahsoka turned. Cato sprinted past the broken table. Padmé scrambled up and grabbed a heavy metal vase. She swung hard, catching Cato full in the face. With a grunt, the bounty hunter fell, smacking her head on the stone floor. She twitched, then lay still.

Ahsoka slid to a halt, lightsabers still at the ready in her hands. Silence descended, broken only by the crackling of flames. Padmé ran to the window and jerked down the burning curtains. She stamped out the flames. The only sounds were the thumps of her feet and her heavy breathing. Finally, the fire was out.

Panting, Padmé walked over to stand next to Ahsoka. Together, they looked down at Cato. Her eyes were closed. She moaned and stirred, then lay still again.

Ahsoka looked at Padmé. "That was a nice trick there, with the vase. You know, you remind me a lot of Anakin sometimes."

Padmé looked down at her white jumpsuit, now scorched and smeared with soot. She reached a hand up to feel her bun, her hair now falling down her back. She smiled. Ahsoka's comment meant a lot to her.

"Thank you, Ahsoka," she said. "May I say, it was my own good luck you were here tonight."

They both looked around at the destroyed apartment. Chunks of broken plates and glass shards lay all over the floor. The wind blew through the window where the bomb had gone through it. The sofa was on its side. Just then, the lighting fixture fell from the ceiling, shattering on the stone floor.

Ahsoka winced. "I'm sorry about the party, Padmé."

Padmé grinned. "Well, it looks like these negotiations will have to be postponed."

Ahsoka laughed, her face relaxing. "In that case, I guess I *will* stay. I'd hate to see all that food go to waste."

Padmé handed her a broom, and together they started to clean up the mess.

A message from Maz:

The tea is almost gone. Soon there will be only wet leaves left in the bottom of the kettle. Here, have the last drop. You have listened to many stories. Oh, thank you. I'll take one last pour. The last bit in the kettle is the strongest. You know, being a hero means . . . stepping forward. No matter the outcome. Aaahh. Perfect tea. Thank you. And thank you for listening to my stories, my friend.

ABOUT THE AUTHOR

EMMA CARLSON BERNE has written many books for children and young adults, including historical fiction, sports fiction, romances, and mysteries. She writes and runs after her three little boys in Cincinnati, Ohio.

LOOK FOR THE NEXT BOOK IN STORES SOON!